World Domination

World Domination

Matthew Edward Petchinsky

World Domination:
Woman's Rule 2: The WAR
By: Matthew Edward Petchinsky

Chapter one

Three months later, everything seemed peaceful, each day was a normal day, Men and women truly worked together as true equals. There was no slavery here or hatred. No violence here, peace and love reign supreme here. Children were not forced to be separated like in the society across the border in the rest of the world.

My farm helped progress the rebel camp, the rebels grew stronger, and the children started to gain better health. We had also moved out of the tents into a fully function city that is well shielded from the elements as well as any attacks. My nanites constructed this city as well as very advanced shield generators for the protection of the city.

Mindy was trained and promoted to be Vice President of the newly formed Rebel Nation. Emerald and Stacy became Secretary of Defense and Secretary of Education as well as running the farm as well. As for me, Alan, I have been appointed as the Architect of All, since it was my nanites that built the city and everything to advance the Rebel camp to a Rebel Nation.

The Rebel leader Roma was promoted to President of the newly formed Rebel Nation. Of course, since we have left the United States, our spies reported that the President was planning an all-out attack on us soon. The spies tell us that she has issued here armies to train and her weapon factories to build a stronger nuclear arsenal.

I had my nanites to build an underground facility full of supplies in case the shield fails. Of course, I don't expect my shields to fail since they are powered by a zero-point energy generator, well about 200 of them. It is amazing what the nanites can build since human minds can imagine it but are limited in their ability to build.

Meanwhile in the war room, Roma, Emerald, Stacy, Mindy, and I were there. We all stood around a table that has maps on the table.

"Are you sure that the shield can withstand any nuclear attack?" Roma asked.

"Yes, the zero-point generator are powerful enough to supply plenty of power to the shield generators." I said fully confident in my nanites ability to build and engineer.

"Look at these images, it appears that The President has issued the building of the Hydrogen bomb." Emerald said pushing the images forward on the table.

"We will be safe behind the shield, but the plasma cannons will wipe anything out that we have mounted on the outside of the shield." I said.

"Let's set up land mines just in case." Mindy said.

"That would be perfect, it will at least slow them down." I said.

We finished our meeting within a hour, when we finished the meeting, we went outside, as we got outside the sun was high in the sky, once the sunlight hit our eyes we all squinted when the bright sun hit our faces, our eyes took a moment to adjust.

When our eyes adjusted to the sunlight, we all looked at the sky, it was a clear blue sky, we looked to the north which is where the command building faced at the north end of the newly built city. We saw the beautiful mountains and forests that we had made peace with the last three months we were here. We all would hate to see such pristine condition. Mindy stood next to me as we looked out over the beautiful scenery, she laid her head on my shoulder and I wrapped my arm around her.

"I don't want to see that view destroyed. I fear this war will destroy it." I said holding Mindy close.

"Me Either, that is why we must do the first strike first." Mindy said.

"NO! we have to have a peaceful solution first, as well as keep the attacks in reserve." I said.

Chapter Two

Meanwhile, back in the United States of America, The President was in her War Room deep below the White House, which is more of a bunker planning on when and where to strike us. She planned on striking our city from all angles, she even thought of even internal sabotage on our city's energy shield generators, but she figured that it wouldn't work because those are well shield as well.

"Mrs. President, we are sending in a group to try and pretend that they are "rebels", our military advisors are still going to try and internally sabotage the generators. Even though, you stand against it, we must try, my apologizes, Mrs. President." The advisor said handing over paperwork to the President.

"That is fine, I guess my title is just a title and it doesn't have any real power." The President said sarcastically taking the paperwork.

"We have learned from our satellite images that the Rebels have several weapons in place to destroy any ground and air assaults." The General said pulling the images up on the big screen holographic television that is in the bunker.

The images were clear and enhanced enough to show all our defenses at the Rebel city. There were even images of our farm and how it was build using nanite technology.

"How do they have these nanites?" The President asked.

"Alan, Mindy's former slave now husband. Before he was a slave, he was a weapons manufacturer as well as inventor. He is very clear according to a report." The General said pulling up my image on the screen.

"I didn't know he was an inventor; I knew he was clever, but an inventor, I couldn't tell. Damn it. If him on their side and those nanites we stand no chance, unless." The President said quickly going to her computer.

The President pulled up my old weapons manufacturing plant. As well as the image of our house.

"Send people to these locations, search them and see what you can find. There is a chance he left some of his research behind." The President said.

"We will send two teams out that way immediately." The General said leaving the War Room.

Meanwhile, back at the Rebel city, I was getting an alert of trespassers on my home property and my manufacturing plant. I pulled up the security footage from both facilities. I saw two military teams searching my home and factory. The first team at my home were in my garage banging up the walls until they found the panel to the underground bunker. They cut some wires and opened the bunker door, which trigger the self-destruct system. The timer pulled up on the screen of my handheld device. The timer was running for five minutes.

The soldiers went in and began to descend the stairs, when they made their way to the first level of the bunker they were breaking and destroying everything, at this point the timer read 2 minutes left, as they were destroying my years of handwork. I watched as they smashed my fridge, dishes and other things, I saw another group go down to level two and destroy all the sleeping quarters, every bed and mattress was ripped up. The timer said one minute left, I watch as my hydroponic garden was obliterated to pieces.

Before long the self-destruct system went off, the security footage cut off. The footage was still live at the manufacturing plant, the team was using a blowtorch to open the door to the bottom levels, which triggered my self-destruct system there too.

Meanwhile, while I was watching, the President got a call that the first team was killed by a self-destruct system. She slammed the phone down in rage.

"Motherfucker!" The President screamed.

I watched at the five-minute timer began at the manufacturing plant. The second team got through the door and were going down the long tunnel as they entered, same thing they were smashing everything. I watched as they progressed down the tunnels searching just like the other team did. The timer was at three minutes and thirty seconds. I watched as they tried to go through my password protected computers, but they smashed the computers since they could not access them.

Before long the second self-destruct system went off and the footage cut off.

When word got back to the President that I had killed the second team as well, she went into a hissy fit of rage. The President thought she was more clever than me, but I proved her wrong. She hated the fact that a man outsmarted her every step of the way. I knew that something like this would have happened, I knew my secrets were well protected.

I closed the device that showed me the security footage and headed to lunch in the large cafeteria building that my nanites built.

Chapter Three

As I entered into the cafeteria building, I saw Emerald, Stacy, and Mindy sitting at a table in the middle of the cafeteria. The saw me and waved me over. I walked over to the table and sat down.

"I have news guys. I know you guys need to hear this." I said.

"What happened?" Mindy said with a look on her face.

Emerald and Stacy had a look of concern on their faces as well.

"It is about our home and my manufacturing plant. The President sent teams to those places to find information about my technology, probably about my nanites." I said.

"Did they find anything?" Emerald said.

"No, the self-destruct system I showed you in the bunker was also in the manufacturing plant. Both teams were killed. My secrets to my technology is safe." I said.

"I'm glad to hear that they didn't get anything of your technology." Mindy said.

"The President is probably angry for you being one step ahead of her." Stacy said.

"Yes, guys we have basically beat her this time." I said getting up to go get some food.

I got ribs, steak, and a baked potato, then I went back to the table. Once I sat down, I began to eat. The ribs were juicy, the flavor washed down my throat. The Steak was medium rare, fat and juicy as well as maple wood smoked. The taste was perfect, I loved the delicious food.

Suddenly, my communicator went off, then Mindy's communicator, then Stacy's communicator, then Emerald's communicator went off. We all got a text that we had some new arrivals that they were claiming they were defectors.

"Looks, like we have some new defectors that just arrived at the gate, not to worry about that, I have a scanner that will tell us if their statements are true." I said as I finished up eating up, then I stood up.

Mindy, Stacy, and Emerald all followed. We all walk to the intake building at the front of the city. As we walked in, we saw six new women that were sitting on chairs, confused on why they were let into the city.

"Excuse me, why haven't we been let into city?" one of the six women asked.

"Well, we need to run a test on each of you. It is standard precaution." I said taking a clipboard from one of the guards.

"What test?" The second women asked.

"Oh, it is nothing. I need you to follow me." I said pointing at the first women in the group.

The woman stood up, and followed me along with two security guards, we walked into a room that had a chair with straps on it. The woman got nervous. I led her into the room.

"Please take a seat." I said.

The woman sat down, and the two guards began to strap her down in the chair. I walked over to her and put a helmet on her head that looked like the old electric chair helmets. I put wires on her arms and legs.

"What is this for?" The woman asked.

"It is to check your vitals." I said as I walked over to a room behind a glass.

I looked at the computer and I saw her heart rate.

"We want to know why you are truly here?" I asked through a microphone.

"We are here for peace, we wanted to get away from the craziness." The woman said.

The computers showed that she was lying.

"Are you working for the President of The United States of America?" I asked.

"No, we are not." The woman said.

The computer showed that she was lying again. I dialed up to machine, and the woman winced in pain.

"It hurts." She said.

"It is fine, it is part of the process. One last question, what are your orders?" I said.

"There are no orders." She lied again.

The machine showed she lied a third time and began to send an electric volt 100,000 watts into the woman's brain, killing her instantly.

I walked out from behind of the glass shield room, went up to the woman's dead body. Stared at it for a moment.

"Dispose of the body, we have other traitors to deal with." I said walking back to the main room.

Before I entered into the main room where the other women were in, I grabbed four disintegrator weapons. I walked back into the main room, gave Emerald, Mindy, and Stacy a weapon. The women looked confused and panicked.

"What is the meaning of this?" One of the women said.

"We know you are here to sabotage us; your sentence is death." I said as I activated the disintegrator weapon, Mindy and the others activated theirs as well.

The women tried to fight and run, but a huge beam came out of the weapons completely disintegrating the women, leaving no trace.

Chapter Four

After we had disintegrated the women that were there to cause harm. Mindy dropped her gun panicking at what she had done, Stacy dropped hers and panicked as well, as did Emerald. I went over to them and hugged each one.

"We had to do this to save what we have built up here." I said holding them.

"I hate killing." Mindy said.

"We are at war, even though the full-scale war hasn't happened yet." I said.

"Violence isn't the answer, though." Stacy said.

"Well, the President of the United States has left us no choice, there is no diplomatic solution but war. Now, I need to talk to our President immediately." I said letting them go and walking out the door.

Mindy and the other followed me soon after, even though it was like thirty seconds apart.

As we walked to the rebel President's home, we saw children playing and enjoying themselves with their fathers in the park that was set up for recreation. It was a beautiful sight. Mindy looked at the sight of it and shed a tear.

"What is it, honey?" I asked.

"I can't believe that the President in the United States wants to destroy all the peacefulness that we built up here." Mindy said tearing up.

I went over to hug her tightly, trying to reassure her.

"We won't let her win. I promise." I said holding Mindy tight.

I held Mindy for a few minutes, then we let each other go and continued on toward the President's house.

Once we arrived at the President's house, I knocked on the door. The President answered the door.

"Yes, Alan? Mindy? Stacy? Emerald? What is going on?" The President said.

"Mrs. President Roma, we have important news, may we come in?" I said.

"Yes, come in." President Roma said opening the door wider letting us in.

We all gathered in her living room. President Roma looked at me.

"Please sit everyone." President Roma said.

We all sat down on her couch she had set in the living room. President Roma sat down as well.

"Okay, give it to me straight, what is the news?" President Roma said.

"Ma'am, we had six women arrive earlier claiming they wanted refuge here, but my scans proved that they were lying and here to sabotage." I said.

"That bitch sent them to cripple our defenses, no doubt." President Roma said.

"Yes, we killed them before they could cause any harm." I said.

"Good, looks like the President over there won't want to be diplomatic, since she is pulling stunts like this." President Roma said.

"Yes, there is another thing she did as well." I said.

"What else happened?" President Roma said.

"Well, she sent two teams to try and recover my technology, but luckily, I had two self-destruct systems in place. She didn't succeed there." I said.

"Damn, she is desperate, I bet she is pissed you have sided with us." President Roma said.

"I agree, Mrs. President Roma, I suggest we go with plan Alpha Sigma Omega." I said.

Mindy, Stacy, and Emerald looked confused at President Roma and I.

"What is Alpha Sigma Omega?" Mindy asked.

Chapter Five

"Alpha Sigma Omega, is an initiative where we send all current nanites to disable everything from internet to all electronic devices as well as vehicles in the United States of America, that will effectively cause them to go into chaos on their end." I said.

"Wait, are you sure you want to do that? Doesn't there have to be a vote first?" Mindy Protested.

"No, only President Roma has to give me the go ahead and I will instruct all nanites to do it." I said.

"Is it morally, right?" Mindy said.

I scoffed and laughed at what Mindy just said, knowing it sounded ridiculous.

"Morally right? We are at war. The President has pushed us to do this. If the shoe was on the opposite foot, they would have done their own Alpha Sigma Omega on us without a question of morality." I said.

"He is right, Mindy. We must do this. There is no other choice." President Roma said.

Mindy looked concerned shook her head.

"Okay, answer me this, if we do this, won't they have possession of your nanites?" Mindy said.

"That is the thing, I have programed the nanites to self-destruct after uploading the program that will cripple their systems, which will cause a series of explosions and a virus that will evolve on its own." I said

"An evolving computer virus? How is that possible?" Mindy said.

"My methods are way more advanced than conventional standards." I said.

"Fine, it is up to you Mrs. President." Mindy said.

President Roma looked at me, then Mindy, then back at me.

"Go ahead, do it. I approve." President Roma said.

"Thank you, Mrs. President Roma." I said pulling out my device that controls my nanites.

I imputed the command, within moment all the nanites in the nation gathered in a large swarm, blocking out the sun. They swarmed like locusts heading south.

Meanwhile, in Washington D.C., The President was getting the last reports in before everything went to a black out. The reports mentioned an extremely large swarm was attacking everything electronic, when the last report came in from New York, The President lost electrical power in the White house. The timing was a bad time, since it was in the middle of July, the White House lost air conditioning and the 110-degree weather was making its way inside heating up the White House.

The President tried to use the phone, but it was not operational, she tried to make her way through the oval office in the somewhat dim lite room, from the little light from the windows. The heat was getting a bit unbearable, the President began to sweat.

Suddenly, outside of the oval office, there were a series of explosions all over the city of Washington D.C., when in fact all over the country there were a large series of explosions from the nanites self-destructing.

By the time, the President made her way outside of the oval office, everything in the hallway was pitch black.

"Hello? Anyone there?" The President said.

No reply. The President gathered the courage to move down the long dark hallway. She knelt down on the floor and begun to crawl like a four-month-old baby trying to find her way, but the darkness was as dark as an obsidian mirror.

Before long, The President made her way to the front door, but not without hitting her head on tables and walls. The President stood up and opened the door, when she made her way outside. She saw the entire city was in a panic.

Chapter Six

Rioting and Fires had broken out from the loss of all internet and electronic. Chaos had begun to ensue.

The President stood there on the White House lawn watching her capital burn. A rage that was building up and kept in a cage like a beast that was being tortured in a zoo, finally broke out. The President looked up at the sky and screamed in rage.

The President felt defeated, but she had a deep secret that no one ever thought of.

Turns out, the President had classic dynamite prepared for an invasion. She had guns that could not be affected to the attack. As for transport she set up horseback riders and regular food soldiers.

Back at the Rebel Nation, my control device indicated that the mission was complete.

"The deed is done. If she has a back up plan it will take her weeks to get here by horse or on foot. Their infrastructure is not repairable for the better part of a decade." I said.

"Let's hope this doesn't come back and bite us in the ass." Mindy said.

"So, there are no more nanites?" Emerald asked.

"Oh no, I always have more, my nanites are self-replicating as well." I said.

"You are full of surprises, aren't you?" Stacy said.

"Well, you guys don't call me the Architect for nothing." I said.

President Roma went over to her home computer and logged into the satellite in orbit. She pulled up an aerial view of the United States, fires were burning across the continent, there was evidence from the aerial scan that everything was in chaos, and it rippled to the rest of the world as well, other countries except us were burning and blacked out.

"Oh wow, your nanites got the rest of the world as well." President Roma said.

"Well, my nanites are very effective." I said.

"What about military instillations?" Stacy asked.

President Roma searched and saw all of the military bases were leveled to rubble.

"Destroyed, gone." President Roma said.

"Well, looks like this war is going to be a fast one." Mindy said.

"Don't underestimate anyone." I said.

Meanwhile, The President had gathered a large group of survivors totaling about 200,000 people. Since she was cut off from the rest of the country, she gathered only a fraction of survivors.

"We will march on the Rebel Nation and squish them like a bug." The President said.

Everyone shouted in excitement. Each one had a pistol, P-90, M-16, and other gun that was available. The President kept hyping them up to get them confident for the invasion.

"As we move north, we will pick up others that will join us in this fight. We must crush the Rebels." The President said.

Everyone shouted in excitement cheering for their victory. The President, however, knew that this campaign was a lost cause because our rebel nation was more superior now, compared to the way they were now. She could not disclose this to the crowd because if they knew they were heading to their deaths.

Within a matter of moments, the 200,000-person army began marching towards our nation from what was left of Washington D.C., none of them realized that they were all about to die a horrible death for a lost cause. The President knew it would take a week to get to our city.

Back in the Rebel City in the Rebel Nation, Mindy, Stacy, Emerald and I were departing President Roma's house.

"Heat sensor scan indicate that a 200,000-person army is headed this way in a week." President Roma said.

"Man, The President over there certainly doesn't give up." I said walking out the door.

"I will see you guys soon; I'm going to rest and have tea." President Roma said closing the door.

Mindy, Stacy, Emerald and I walked to the park. I grabbed each of their hands, and we stood in a circle staring at each other.

"Let's vow that whatever happens, none of us become blood thirsty from the killings." I said.

"Agreed." Mindy said gripping my hand tighter.

"I definitely agree." Stacy said.

"Agreed 100%" Emerald said.

Chapter Seven

Meanwhile, around the outskirts of Washington D.C., the President and her every growing army has doubled from 200,000 to 400,000 person army. The President knew she would have a large army, but even though their numbers were to grow large in number, it was basically leading sheep to the slaughter. The President did not disclose to the unsuspecting participants that they would surely all die.

They march on, picking up those that were lost and confused. Indoctrinating them in the ranks of the ever-growing army.

Back in our rebel nation, I was in my lab building more nanites, but these nanites were flesh eating nanites. If we lose this war, these nanites would be released to destroy all human life. I also built sensors to detect if everyone in our city was killed, the sensors would break vials of these nanites to be released immediately. I kept this project secret of course; I wasn't sure if President Roma would approve. Mindy certainly wouldn't approve.

My communicator rang, I answered, it was Mindy.

"Alan, we need you in the war room." Mindy said.

"I'll be there shortly." I said hanging up.

I set the computer in my lab to mass produce the flesh eating nanites and place them in vials. As I stepped out of my lab, I went straight to the war room.

Once I arrived, Mindy, Emerald, Stacy and President Roma were there. They had on the big screen monitor as infrared scan of the northeastern coast of the United States. Mindy had a look of worry on her face. The scan showed that The President of the United States had gathered over 950,000-person army headed our way.

"Looks like the President over there has been gathering quite a force over there, and it is ever growing." President Roma said with concern in her voice.

"Well, we should be well protected, remember they will have only regular guys no missiles or nukes. Our weaponry will slaughter them all." I said.

"But what if they cause our city to fall?" Emerald said looking at me for guidance.

Everyone looked at me for guidance, I say the look of fear and worry on their faces.

"Alright, I wasn't going to say anything, but I am developing fleshing nanites." I said.

"Flesh eating nanites? Isn't that immoral?" Mindy said.

"I knew you were going to say that. Look if the city falls these nanites will kill the rest of the human race in the entire planet, we cannot let their society exist." I said.

Mindy, Emerald, Stacy and President Roma looked at me if I am insane, but then they looked at each other.

"Well, you are right, if the city falls our rebellion will be for nothing and future generations will suffer in that new society. I approve of your plan even though I don't fully agree with it. I hate the way society has gotten now." President Roma said.

Chapter Eight

Meanwhile, the President and her ever growing army got closer to the city, she had nearly two million persons. One of the nights that they stopped in a very dense forested area, the President snuck away from the camp, deep in the dark woods. She looked around.

"Okay, let's speak. We are alone." The President said.

A dark figure appeared, it was a woman with horns on her head, she had pale white skin with feathers, her name is Hecate.

"You are doing well by gathering more to fight and sacrifice, but I must warn you. The rebels have in place a plan to kill every living human if the rebel city falls." Hecate said.

"Can't you help us win?" The President said.

"No, you must solve this yourself, but do you want to know who it is that created a weapon to kill everyone?" Hecate said.

"Alan? What weapon?" The President said

Hecate nodded.

"Flesh eating nanites. Bastet protects him. He cannot be killed." Hecate said.

"Well, can't you fight Bastet?" The President said.

"I could but she is more powerful than I." Hecate said.

"So, you are a coward." The President said laughing.

Hecate got offend and grabbed the President by the throat.

"Don't test me. I may not be able to fight Bastet, but I can kill you human." Hecate said squeezing The President's throat piercing her throat a little with her claws.

Hecate released her grip on The President's throat. The President fell to the ground coughing and gasping for air.

"I still need you to lead these sacrifices to the slaughter. I won't kill you, but I hope you learned to not be insolent." Hecate said disappeared into the darkness of the night.

The President gathered her strength to stand up, coughed and walked back to camp.

When the President made it back to the camp, she was limping a bit. One of the guards saw her limping, she quickly ran over to the President.

"Mrs. President, what happened to you?" The guard said grabbing the President to support her from the limping. The guard also noticed that there were claw marks on her neck.

"I am fine." The President said trying to seem weak.

The President and the Guard went to the infirmary tent. The doctor was shocked that the President was injured.

"What happened?" The doctor asked rushing to the President's side and laying her on a cot.

The President didn't want to tell the truth about what had really happened, so she quickly came up with a lie.

"A group of wild men attacked me while I was out in the woods trying to chart our position in the stars." The President lied.

"I will gather a team and go hunt them down, Mrs. President." The Guard said turning to leave the infirmary tent.

The President knew they would find nothing, but at least she didn't have to tell them the truth that they are all sheep heading for the slaughter.

Meanwhile, in the heavens, the Gods and Goddesses observed from above. Hecate was there watching her group of players. Bastet was watching her group of players as well.

"Well, looks like we are about to see a slaughter either way. Either Alan murders millions or billions with the nanites, or my group crushes your group and then the slaughter of billions begins. I can't wait to see this happen." Hecate said excited.

"You really like death and destruction, don't you?" Bastet said.

"Yes, I live for it." Hecate said.

Bastet turned to leave quickly, disappearing away.

Down on Earth in the rebel nation, I was in the middle of producing more flesh eating nanites. Mindy, Emerald and Stacy were in my lab with me.

"You know this is morally wrong." Mindy said.

I looked away from my computer for a moment and turned to Mindy. I gave her a look like as if she was being ridiculous.

"Honey, this is war. They stopped being morally right a long time ago. I know killing billions is wrong, but so is slaughtering us all for their unethical and unmoral ways of life." I said turning back to the computer putting in the final command to mass produce more flesh eating nanites.

Mindy stared at me, then at Emerald and then Stacy.

"Can't you guys help me convince him that he needs not do this?" Mindy said.

Emerald and Stacy both looked at each other for a moment then back at Mindy.

"We agree with Alan, he is right." Emerald said.

Mindy scoffed and her face got flushed with red.

"What the hell? Why don't we just crack the earth in half while we are at it!" Mindy said angered that Emerald and Stacy were on my side.

I turned and stood up and walked over to Mindy and hugged her.

"My love, I know how you feel, but how about this. I am thinking that we should have another set of nanites create life once the flesh-eating ones kill off all life?" I said.

"What are you playing God now? You can't do that. You cannot just kill all life then recreate life." Mindy said.

"I am speaking practically. If we have a second group of program nanites to rebuild the human species, what harm would that do?" I said.

"You are not God. I got to go clear my head." Mindy said storming out of my lab as fast as she could.

Chapter Nine

I followed Mindy trying to keep up with her. When I caught up with her outside of my lab, I grabbed her arm.

"Unhand me, don't touch me! Fuck you!" Mindy said struggling to get out of my grip.

I pulled Mindy towards me hugging her trying to calm her down. Mindy was fighting and struggling to get away from me.

"Mindy, calm down. We must do this for the sake of the human race." I said holding her tightly to me.

"It is morally wrong. You have lost your mind." Mindy said still struggling against me.

"We are at war, my nanites will rewrite the human genome and create equality." I said.

Mindy stopped struggling, took a deep breathe, then looked me deep into my eyes.

"I know both views are wrong, but isn't there has to be another way." Mindy said.

I placed my hand on her cheek, looked her deep in her eyes.

"I assure you, there is no other way, my love." I said.

Mindy sighed.

"Fine, do what you have planned. It has to be an honorable death for you and I honestly, instead of us being slaughter like an animal." Mindy said holding me tight.

Meanwhile, back at the camp where the President and her army is, just outside a major metro area. The President was in the infirmary tent sleeping when Hecate appeared to her in a dream.

"What are you doing in me dream?" The President asked.

"I can do as I please, enter in any dream I wish, wherever I wish. Now, I have a task for you and your army." Hecate said.

"What is this task?" The President said.

"There is an armory about five miles away from her full of nuclear waste, collect most of it and catapult them into the rebel city." Hecate said.

"Catapult? How are we to do that? We have no catapults" The President said.

Hecate in her annoyance struck the President across the face. The President fell to the ground.

"You can build them or use the one prebuilt in the armory, dummy." Hecate said.

The President collected herself and stood up, facing Hecate.

"Alright, we will do it." The President said bowing her head to Hecate.

Hecate grinned a mischievous grin.

"Good, serve me well and you will be well rewarded." Hecate said turning and leaving into the smoke of the dream.

The President woke up gasping, a nurse walked over to her.

"What is wrong, Mrs. President?" The nurse said.

The President sat up on her cot and placing her hands on her face, then in a downward motion wiping them downward, then turning to the nurse.

"Can you summon my advisors and military leaders? I have a destination for us to move on to." The President said.

"I will go get them." The nurse said turning and leaving the tent.

Sitting there in her cot, the President knew that Hecate was right and she was nothing more that a pawn of hers. A cold chill went down The President's spine.

Chapter Ten

Ten minutes later, the President's military advisors arrived into the infirmary tent.

"Yes, Mrs. President? You summoned us?" One of the advisors said.

"Yes, I had a dream about an armory five miles from her full of nuclear waste and catapults. We need to set up a convoy to collect them and we will had a weapon we can use again the rebel city." The President said.

The advisors looked at the President in silence for a moment, then looked at each other, then back at the President.

"Okay, we will gather a group and head that way. We will need to meet up with us after we gather the weapons. Tell us how you came to learn of such weapons?" An advisor said.

"It was in a dream message from Hecate." The President said.

"Ah, blessed be the Goddesses Hecate." The advisor said.

"You are a leader as well as a prophet to us." The advisor said bowing to the President.

"Thank you, let me hand pick those that will go gather the weapons." The President said getting off the cot in the infirmary tent.

"Mrs. President, I feel you are not ready for such activity, please lay back down." The nurse said grabbing the President's arm.

The President quickly snapped her arm away from the nurse.

"I feel fine. I am strong enough to walk and carry myself." The President said looking at the nurse firmly in the eye.

"My apologizes, Ma'am." The nurse said backing up from the President.

"Mrs. President, we as your advisors can handle the selection process, we agree that you are ready to move yet." The advisor said.

The President looked sharply at her advisors, a rage started to build inside her.

"I am feeling well enough, I am not weak. If I hear your 'disapproval' again and telling me what I can and cannot do. I will have you personally shot in front of the whole camp." The President Threaten.

The advisor gulped in nervousness, hoping that she wouldn't upset The President.

"My apologizes, Mrs. President. I was out of place." The advisor said turning her eyes to the ground not making eye contact with the President.

The President grinned at the sight of her submissive subordinate subject, much like a dominatrix mistress with her submissive slave. The President walked forward and went outside of the infirmary tent.

She cleared her throat as she began to shout for the whole camp to hear her.

"Attention! Everyone! I have an announcement to make!" The President shouted.

Everyone in the camp was gathering around the President.

"I had a vision from our great Goddess Hecate! She has shown me a base where there are weapons we can use that is located five miles to the west of our current position." The President said.

"All hail mother Hecate" The large crowd said in unison.

"We need a volunteer group of twenty followers to gather the weapons and meet us twelve miles away from our current position. Once we have these weapons, we will continue our march onto the rebel city. We are one hundred miles from their city." The President said.

"What are these weapons?" One of the followers in the crowd asked.

The President looked towards her. The young twenty year old girl was standing in the front of the crowd. She had almond skin and beautiful black hair.

"What is your name?" The President asked as she pointed at the young woman.

"My name is Amber. I ask again, what are these weapons you speak of?" Amber asked.

The President grinned and shook her head.

"Amber, if you must know, these weapons are catapults and radioactive waste." The President said.

"Are you insane? You are going to have us all killed before we can attack the rebels. Radioactive waste is not a great weapon, especially with limited...." A gun shot went off killing Amber before she could finish her speech.

The President then blew at the opening of a Beretta 9mm pistol. Amber fell to the ground dead.

"Anyone else has any objections?" the President asked holstering the gun.

The crowd remained quiet, then twenty volunteers came forward in fear of the President.

Chapter Eleven

Meanwhile, back in the Rebel city, I was following Mindy to go speak with President Roma. Mindy was silent during the entire walk over to the President's home. I could see from the expression on her face that she was still bothered by the fact that I have created a weapon to kill all life. I know that my trying to calm her down didn't work as well as I had hoped.

As we walked up the steps to President Roma's home, I knocked on the door. President Roma opened the door, she was in a green satin robe and lingerie type of clothing since she was relaxing.

"What is it, Alan?" President Roma asked looking at me.

"I wanted to tell that the flesh eating nanites are ready. Also, there is another option for us after they had done their job. I can create a second batch of nanites to recreate life. Are you okay with that?" I asked.

President Roma stepped outside in her robe and green lingerie. She crossed her arms and raised an eyebrow.

"Won't this cycle start all over again and be like it is now?" President Roma asked with concern in her voice.

"Not necessarily, these nanites can create a better human species, one where they have no hate, not anger, no jealousy, no negative emotions. Just love, compassion and a sense to work together." I said.

President Roma took a deep breath, and let out a hard long sigh.

"Look, Alan your technology has helped us greatly, I just don't know if that is the moral thing to do." President Roma said noticing Mindy's look.

"That is what I told him, President Roma. I find it as if he is playing God." Mindy said.

"I understand, where both of you are coming from, but I would like to see this world in better hands." I said.

"I am sorry, Alan the answer is no. We have no right to create a new human race after you nanite kill all human life." President Roma said.

I shook my head in agreement, but I knew that neither of them could see this from the greater vision than I can. I planned in secret from that very moment to go ahead with my plan. I am after all the Great Architect.

Mindy and I wished President Roma a pleasant evening, as we both turned to leave. Mindy turned to me, grabbing my shoulder roughly.

"I knew she would not approve of the second half of your plan. Let's go home and eat dinner. We need to keep an eye on the monitors to see what our enemy is up to." Mindy said.

Mindy and I walked home, but I kept my mouth shut on what my plan was. While she slept, I would work at night on the nanites that would rebuild human life. I knew it would have to be done.

When we got home, Mindy went to the kitchen to cook some hamburger meat for dinner for hamburger patties without the bread. While I went to the living room, where our big screen tv was, which can become a monitor as well. I pulled out the keyboard, typed in a command pulling up the satellite scan. The scan showed the President's army had gathered about twenty miles from the Canadian border, and a group of about twenty were on an army base five miles from their camp.

I enhanced the scan, which revealed that the base had catapults and there were radioactive signatures indicating radioactive waste on the base. My eye grew wide from what the live feed showed me that they were gathering the catapults and radioactive waste to weaponize against us.

"Mindy! Come here quick! Get President Roma on the phone. Along with Stacy and Emerald! We have a huge problem!" I shouted logging on to my lab's production program to write a program to create nanites that eat the radioactive materials and the catapults.

Mindy came to see what was going on and she was shocked at what she saw. Mindy picked up the phone and called President Roma, Stacy and Emerald to call for an emergency meeting.

Chapter Twelve

About 45 minutes later, President Roma, Stacy and Emerald showed up at our house for the emergency meeting. I had the monitor still monitoring their movements. Also, had a screen on the progress of my new type of nanites.

Everyone looked at the monitor in disbelief.

"Good thing you discovered this. I see you are working on a new type of nanite to consume the radioactive waste and the catapults." President Roma said pointing out the obvious.

"Yes, since I am responsible for the defenses of this nation of ours, especially the city." I said.

"Can't our shields protect us?" Stacy said.

"Yes, for a little while, but the radiation could leak through. I would give it about a 36% chance of radiation leakage." I said.

"36% chance of radiation leaking through? Then what is the point of the shield if it can't protect us fully from radiation as well!" Stacy said getting irritated.

"We will still be protected; it is just radiation isn't solid matter that can be fully protected from. Remember it is hard to be 100% protected from something without physical form." I said making perfect sense.

Mindy, Stacy, Emerald and President Roma remained silent, so not to feel dumb by the next thing they might say. I saw that everyone in the room felt dumb compared to me.

Emerald broke the silence.

"Are we well-armed to fight them off?" Emerald asked.

"Yes, but I would like to place landmines around the city of these new type of nanites." I said.

"How long will it take to install those?" President Roma asked.

"24 hours." I said.

Mindy, Stacy, Emerald and President Roma were silent, they all stared at one another then back at me.

"We will get a group of volunteers to help execute your plan, Alan." President Roma said.

"Thank you, I appreciate it." I said.

"I can't believe that this war is going to end soon. This is one of the fastest wars in history, since you introduced your nanites, Alan." Emerald said with a shocked tone in her voice.

I looked at Emerald and the others, shook my head, as I put my hands to my sides.

"I had to do something, it is the best option, either get slaughtered or fight back." I said.

President Roma stood up from where she was sitting, walked over to me, put her hands on my shoulders. Looked at me in the eyes. Her beautiful brown eyes stared deep into my soul.

"We appreciate you, Alan. You are loved here by all these people. Everyone is grateful for the life you have given them these last few months, no one will blame you for your nanites slaughtering us all to protect our way of life." President Roma said moving her hands to my cheeks, still staring into my eyes.

Mindy watched, but didn't get jealous, since we had become like family with President Roma and her people. President Roma kissed me passionately on the lips. I was shocked that she was kissing me, then Stacy and Emerald each took their turns kissing me passionately. I believe it was to show that I was not doing the wrong thing and they still loved me.

"I love you guys, you are my family, I hope things will be great for us in the afterlife." I said heading over to the computer to check the progress on the nanite production.

Chapter Thirteen

Meanwhile, about twenty miles outside of the Canadian border, The President was in her tent sitting on her cot. She was holding a photo of Mindy and I. She was tearing up because she had a deep love for both Mindy and I. She wished deep down that things were different. It hurts her that she would have to kill Mindy and I.

Hecate appeared to her.

"Are you skulking over those worthless creatures?" Hecate said taunting her.

The President wiped the tears from her eyes and looked up at Hecate.

"Yes, I deeply love them. I don't want them to be killed." The President protested confessing her love for us.

"You are weak, sentimental, pathetic. The only reason your are in this position of power is because of me." Hecate insulted her.

The President's face turned red out of anger, but she could not do anything or say anything to Hecate to defend herself. She was powerless.

"What do you want?" The President asked.

"I came to inform you, the rebels know of your new weapons and that Alan prick has created nanites to destroy the new weapons you have. I honestly, do not know what you can do to help you." Hecate lied.

Hecate wanted to see everyone to be slaughtered with the nanites. Death is her paradise.

"Crap, I have no choice, we must keep pushing forward. I have everyone counting on me." The President said.

Hecate smirked a devious smirk just before disappearing.

Hecate had the tools in place, she knew that everything would end, Bastet on the other hand had another plan in place to have Alan create nanites to rebuild human life. Soon the players will take their places and this war will end and life as they know it.

The President stepped outside of her tent into the night, it was a calm night. Everyone in the camp was asleep. You could hear crickets in the woods all around the camp. The President looked up at the sky, she saw every star in the night sky clearly. The stars were diamonds of the sky, and mesmerizing just like they were thousands of years ago.

A shooting star strung across the sky. The President made a wish upon the star. She wished that this war would end, but for her, Mindy and I to be spared.

Back in the rebel city, I was with a group of volunteers placing out and burying large barrels of nanites around the perimeter of the rebel city, but these were specially designed barrels with built in sensor to detect a change in land weight and movement. I will remotely activate the sensors once I get back to my lab to prevent any accidents.

"Sir, we have completed or tasks we are heading back into the city." A group said over the radio.

"Okay, copy that." I said.

"Our tasks are done too." Group 2 said over the radio.

"Same here." Group 3 said.

"Same here." Group 4 said.

"Okay guys, thank you for your help." I said over the radio finishing off my work.

After I finished my task, I went back inside the city, Mindy was waiting for me holding a tablet.

"According to our aerial and heat scans, the barrels are perfectly placed to protect the city." Mindy said handing me the tablet.

"Perfect, we should be well protected now." I said.

I walked up behind Mindy, wrapped my arms around her, holding her tight. Mindy reached behind her and placed her hand on my cheek. She smiled and turned around, looked at me deep in my eyes, then she kissed me passionately. I kissed her passionately back, I placed my arms around her and brought her in close. My hands moved down her back as we kissed. Her hands moved around my hips.

We broke from kissing to breath. We stared at one another for a moment. Still with a lustful urge in the air.

"Let's go have sex it has been a while." Mindy said.

I grabbed Mindy and picked her up, carrying her to a small room in the back of the lab that had a bed there. I laid her down on the bed and began to kiss her again, Mindy was undoing my belt from my pants as I was kissing her, I began kissing her down her neck, moving down her body. I pulled her shirt off and kissed her 34b sized breasts, her beautiful almond skin, I removed her bra, I sucked he breasts and nipples. Mindy let out a moan from the pleasure of the sucking. I kept kissing her down to her belly, until I got to her pants. I undid you pants and removed both her pant and panties exposing her beautiful almond Vagina. I moved my head towards her Vagina and began to kiss it, suck and tongue her Vagina. Mindy let out a loud moan from the pleasure. Mindy shoved my head deep into her Vagina. She came, then I got up and took my pants off and boxers exposing my rock hard erection. Mindy got up, moved toward me, grabbed my penis with her right hand and began to stroke it as she moved her mouth towards to head of my penis, sticking out her tongue and slowly teasing my penis head, I shivered from the pleasure. Mindy noticed and went slower. She knew she was causing me to get eager.

After a few minutes, she had worked her way to have my entire 6.5inch penis deep in her mouth. She bobbed her head as she sucked and jerked my penis, I enjoyed the feeling. Within a few minutes, I ejaculated on her face. Mindy laugh as she grabbed my boxers and wiped her face off, grabbing ahold of my penis to keep it erect. She stood up and laid me down on the bed and she got onto my erect penis. She inserted my penis inside her Vagina and let out a moan as she enjoyed the feeling of it inside her.

She began to thrust into me, I felt a sense of euphoria and pleasure from her thrusts, I leaned up wrapping my arms around her as she thrusted, her beautiful breasts were in my face, I grabbed them and squeezed them, I suck them in my mouth and began to suck them. Mindy moaned in pleasure.

After 20 minutes, we both ejaculated at the same time. Mindy collapsed on the bed in a euphoric feeling and out of breath.

I turned to look at her face to face, she and I looked into each other's eye caressing each other's faces.

"I love you, Alan." Mindy said still staring at me.

"I love you too, Mindy," I said still caressing her face.

Chapter Fourteen

The President and her army were moving closer to the Rebel city. I monitored them on the satellite scan. They were less than a day away from the city. I was in my lab, putting the final touches on the nanites that will recreate life.

"Alan, are you seeing on the scan?" Mindy said over the radio.

"Yes, I see they are a day way from us. Is everyone prepared for the battle?" I replied back.

"Yes, we are all prepared." Emerald said over the radio.

"Yes, we are prepared as well." Stacy said over the radio as well.

"We will fight until our last man and women." President Roma Said over the radio.

"My technology will ensure that won't happen, but it is good that we are prepared for anything." I said and reassured everyone over the radio.

The scanner showed that the President and her army stopped to camp half a day away from the camp.

"Alan, I have a plan." Mindy said.

"Let's have a preemptive strike to them before they attack us." Mindy said over the radio.

"That is a good plan. How about a drone strike?" Stacy suggested.

I put my hands on my face in disappointment.

"I thought you wanted a peaceful solution, Mindy?" I said over the radio.

"Yes, but they are leaving us no choice now, we must strike first. At least take out a few numbers of theirs. According to the scan we are facing 86 million of them." Mindy said over the radio.

"Alright, I will set up a few drones with missiles for the strike. It will be ready in one hour." I said over the radio getting up from my desk heading to our drone storage but taking the radio with me.

"That is a great plan." President Roma said over the radio.

Meanwhile, just a few miles outside or rebel city. The President and her army were camping and preparing for the attack, but they needed to rest from the long journey that was on foot.

"Mrs. President, do you want us to send out a scout team to scope out the perimeter?" One of the military advisors suggested.

"No, it is night. The scouts won't see anything. Plus we don't know the terrain either, they could get lost at night and won't make it back alive." The President said.

"Okay, Ma'am." The advisor said.

The military advisor secretly, went behind the President's back and sent a scout of four to scope the Rebel city. The President was right, the scouts didn't return, but not for the reason you might think.

Hecate slaughtered the scouts the moment they were a mile away from the camp. Hecate wanted to ensure a full slaughter on both sides and no information on either side.

Back in the rebel city, I had prepared three drones for a drone strike. I launched the drones right away.

As the drones moved towards to the President's camp, I watched the tracking on the screen.

Back at the President's camp, The President stepped out of her tent when she noticed the noise of the drones. She looked up at the sky.

"Everyone Run! It is a drone strike!" The President screamed, but it was too late the first wave of the strike hit fast.

Explosions were all over the camp, The President was knocked to the ground from the shock of the explosions. Millions were screaming in agony and pain. Strike two took out the catapults, and a few more. The drones were unarmed, and they returned to the Rebel city.

I looked at the scan and it showed that the strike had killed about 5 million and only 5 million injured.

"The strike didn't work as well as I had hoped." Mindy said over the radio.

"I know, but at least we weakened them a bit. Especially, taking out their weapons." I said over the radio.

Chapter Fifteen

The President was dazed and looking all around her camp in flames with her people screaming in agony. Her military advisor ran up to the President, who was with a neutral face, it struck fear into the advisor. Deep down the President was screaming and cursing.

"Ma'am, we have 5 million of us dead, another 5 million wounded. The catapults are destroyed. What are your orders, Ma'am?" The Military advisor said.

The President keep a neutral face, she kept looking all around the camp that was in flames. Then she turned to her advisor.

"Tend to the wounded we will attack at dawn." The President ordered.

The President went to a secluded area of the camp, there waiting for her was Hecate in a black cloak covering her face and body.

"First blood has been shed. I took care of the scouts that your advisor sent out behind your back, kill her." Hecate said disappearing.

The President was enraged, she turned and went to her tent, grabbed a large bladed knife. Then went up to her advisor who was assisting a wounded soldier.

The advisor turned to look at the President noticing the knife in her hand.

"Mrs. President, what is it? Why are you holding the knife?" The advisor said with fear in her voice.

"Did you order a scout team behind my back? Be honest." The President said gripping the knife tightly.

"Yes, your judgement is.." The advisor stopped midsentence with a knife through her throat, the President pulled it out fast and the advisors body hit the ground hard.

The President then walked up to the wounded soldier and slit her throat as well. The President went through the camp slaughtering those that were wounded since they would only hold the army back.

By dawn, The President and her army had collected themselves and began marching towards the Rebel city. The President had a rage the was burning hotter than any sun. She wanted vengeance upon me and my fellow rebels. She wanted my head as a trophy.

"Guys, they are moving, looks like they slaughtered their wounded. I am not reading any wounded soldiers left behind." I said over the radio while typing in the defense system codes to arm it.

"That is expected." President Roma said over the radio.

"Let's get everyone armed before they show up." I said over the radio.

"Already on it!" Stacy said over the radio.

I prepare an entire fleet of drones to be launched in case the shield fails, they would drop the nanites to reconstitute life. After I finished making the final preparations, I went outside my lab.

What I didn't know was that Hecate was in my lab. She moved stealthily around making her way to the computer. She typed in a command code to cause an overload in the shield emitters and the power sources as well. Hecate would not let anyone live, she made sure the shield would fail at the right moment that way there would be a slaughter.

As I made my way outside, Mindy was already waiting for me.

"They are a mile out. We are all ready to fight." Mindy said.

"This shield should hold and those weapons up there should be able to hold them back." I said.

The President and her army were pushing further through the woods until they were just outside the city. The President looked upon our walls that were 100 feet tall. She felt her rage spread forth like a flame thrower.

"Someone give me a bazooka!" The President ordered.

One of her soldiers hand her a bazooka, she took it and signaled for the over bazooka and as well RPG holders to line up.

"Fire!" The President ordered.

The projectiles were flying through the air until they were stopped by the Energy shield.

“"Reload." The President said.

Chapter Sixteen

"Fuck, they are not moving towards the land mines yet. Also according to my scans, the shield is getting close to failing. It doesn't make sense. I doubled checked my system before this started." I said panicking a bit.

Mindy looked at me in disbelief.

"I think the universe wants a slaughter." Mindy said.

Actually, Mindy wasn't wrong about that, it was the Goddesses Hecate that truly wanted the slaughter. My perimeter defenses were firing off when the sixth set of explosives hit the shield. We could hear screams on the other side of the wall.

The President still was having the shield being bombarded by bazooka and RPG explosives.

Meanwhile, my shield emitters were being over whelmed under the constant stress of the bombardment(plus Hecate had weakened them). The Emitters exploded, causing the shield to fail and shake the city that it sound like a bell and a shockwave, we all inside fell to the ground.

The President saw the shield fail and she screamed at her army to charge the city. I was getting to my feet, confused. I helped Mindy, President Roma, Stacy and Emerald to their feet.

"Something isn't right. That should not have happened. Everyone Defensive positions now!" I said running to get to a weapon.

A series of bazooka shells took out our defensive guns, causing large explosions. As the Presidents army were charging towards the city from all angles, the second they hit the perimeter land mines they exploded open cause 40 or fifty to fall all around the perimeter, but the nanites began to attack them and eat their flesh a large cloud of them took out about 5 million on all five sides, but the army kept pushing through it. The President had seven of her RPG soldiers to take out the front gate of the city, The nanites were still swarming around, but The President still survived that and cause the front gates to fall.

Mindy and I along with forty others were knocked on the ground from the explosion of the from gate. I got to my feet just as the President and her soldiers were storming through along with the nanites that were eating their flesh and attacking our people.

They looked like zombies running towards you as they were with swords and regular gun killing us. I grabbed Mindy's arm, and we ran to my lab.

President Roma was killed by being shot in the head by the President. Stacy and Emerald were shot by her as well.

"Mindy! Alan! Come get your punishment!" The President shouted as she was making her way like a demon on a war path.

Mindy and I made our way to my lab. I quickly went to the computer and saw that my system had been tampered with.

"Someone tampered with my system, that is why the shield failed. Who could tamper with it? I have it password protected." I said

"It doesn't matter now, what are you going to do?" Mindy said.

"I am going to overload the power sources, it will destroy everything." I said programming the overload to go off in five minutes, but I set the drones to launch to leave the area to recreate life.

The door to my lab exploded. The President walked in with rage on her face, she shot me in the shoulder. I fell to the ground, grabbing my shoulder.

"Ahhh!!!" I shouted in agony.

"Alan!" Mindy shouted and froze in place as the President was heading towards us.

Chapter Seventeen

The President pointed a guy towards Mindy's head.

"Hello, Mindy. We meet again." The President said as the nanites were eating away at her face, blood was dripping.

"We surrender, please don't kill us." Mindy pleaded.

I was still by the computer crawling to get to my keyboard, but the President didn't notice.

"Surrender? Hahaha. Don't make me laugh. It is too late for that." The President said pointing a gun at Mindy's head, but she wasn't focusing well since the nanites were eating her brain.

"Please put the weapon don't. I will be with you, I promise." Mindy said.

"Be with me? No, too late for that. You joined the rebels and Alan is needing to die too. Men need to die!" The President said as her flesh was falling off her body.

Mindy moved closer hoping to grab the gun before she could fire. I on the other hand made the overload going sooner now, the President noticed I was still alive and turned her attention to me and pointed the gun at me, firing square in my chest.

"NO!!!!" Mindy screamed as she knocked the gun out of the President's gun out of her hands.

They got into a fist fight, but the President was too weak from the nanites eating her flesh. While Mindy had the President on the ground she ran over to me and picked up my head, there was blood everywhere. She was cry, holding me close. She then noticed that my hand was on the enter key and the over load was three seconds away. Mindy went down and kissed me as the power source was over loading, causing a large explosion that took out the entire city and releasing more nanites that were like locusts heading all over the world, eating everything living in site.

The nanites, had consumed everything living withing a matter of six hours all life had ceased to exist. As for the drones, they released three hours after the last human died. Those nanites set out to rebuild life, animal, human and wipe evidence of our bad society.

The human cycle rebuilt. These humans will not know of our mistake. They will be better with no hatred, prejudice, no greed. The nanites will program their minds better and souls to be pure.

The End